8/05
D0566051

by NANCY CASTALDO

illustrated by

MÉLISANDE POTTER

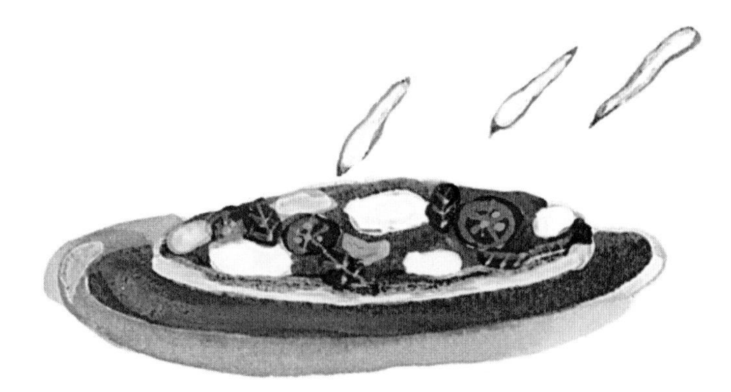

Holiday House / New York

For Dean, my true love,
who shares my passion for pizza
N. C.

My thanks to Pia Giselle Kier
Chloe George Inas Anni Claude
for peaceful places to paint pizzas
M. P.

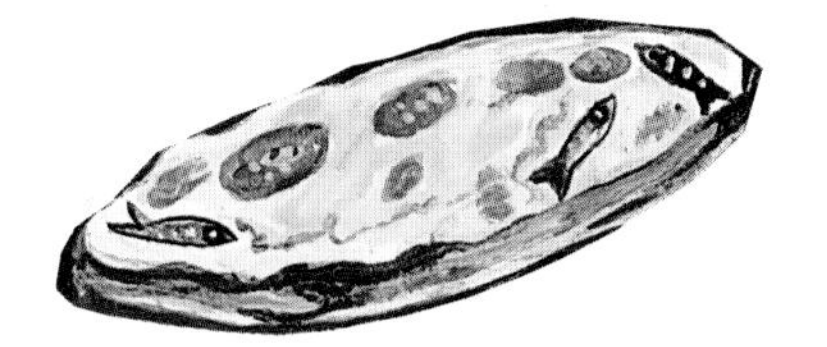

Printed in the United States of America
www.holidayhouse.com
First Edition
1 3 5 7 9 10 8 6 4 2

Library of Congress Cataloging-in-Publication Data
Castaldo, Nancy F. (Nancy Fusco), 1962–
Pizza for the queen / by Nancy Castaldo;
illustrated by Mélisande Potter.—1st ed.
p. cm.
Summary: In 1889 Napoli, Italy, Raffaele Esposito prepares a special
pizza for the queen. Based on a true story. Includes a recipe.
ISBN 0-8234-1865-0
[1. Pizza—Fiction. 2. Naples (Italy)—History—1860–1945—Fiction.
3. Italy—History—1870–1914—Fiction.] I. Potter, Mélisande, ill. II. Title.
PZ7.C268585Pi 2005
[E]—dc22
2004058134

ISBN-13: 978-0-8234-1865-7
ISBN-10: 0-8234-1865-0

Like most June days in Napoli, the eleventh day of the year 1889 was warm and clear. Already at nine o'clock in the morning Raffaele Esposito knew the day would be busy. The days always were. Everyone loved his pizza, and he loved making it.

The streets that morning were like every other morning. Fishermen sold their catch. Women carried jugs of mineral water for sale. Farmers arrived with carts of fruits and vegetables ripened in the sun. The smell of baking bread filled the air.

Raffaele had bought the pizzeria called Pietro e Basta Così from the original owner, Pietro; and to make things simple he kept the name. After all, the pizzeria was quite famous in Napoli.

Inside Pietro e Basta Così, Raffaele set to work making the dough for his pizza. He was so busy kneading that he did not see the gentleman come into the pizzeria.

"I hear that you make the best pizza in all of Napoli," the man said to Raffaele.

Raffaele looked up to see the queen's messenger standing before him. "*Sì*," said Raffaele. After all, who was he to argue with such an important gentleman?

"Her Majesty Queen Margherita has heard her servants speak of your pizza and would like to taste what all the fuss is about," he said. "I will come back around seven o'clock this evening for a pizza for the queen."

Raffaele's eyes got very wide. What an honor to make a pizza for the queen! "It will be my pleasure," he said, bowing to the gentleman.

Then he felt his heart beat faster. "What pizza shall I make?"

Would the queen like a pizza with little fish? Would the queen like a pizza with cheese? Perhaps she might like artichokes. Raffaele could not decide. Then he had a brilliant idea. Why not give her a choice?

Raffaele closed the pizzeria and set out to collect the finest ingredients. After all, the queen must have the best.

First he stopped to see Giovanni, the cheese seller.

"Giovanni, the queen has asked for my pizza. I must have your best cheese," said Raffaele.

"It is a great honor for me to know that the queen will taste my cheese," said Giovanni. "Let me see. Would she like this creamy fontina, or perhaps this fine, blue Gorgonzola from Milano that smells like the feet of a king?"

GIOVANNI'S FORMAGGIO

"Giovanni, what about your mozzarella? It is the best in all of Napoli."

"I cannot give the queen the mozzarella di Bufala. It is for peasants."

"But, Giovanni, the queen wants to taste the pizza I make for the people of Napoli. I make it with the mozzarella." And with that Raffaele selected some creamy white balls of mozzarella and put them in his sack.

Giovanni just shook his head as Raffaele walked away.

Next Raffaele stopped to purchase olive oil from Maria. "*Buongiorno*, Maria, I must have your finest olive oil for a pizza for Queen Margherita."

"A *pizza* for Queen Margherita? But she can have any food she likes!" said Maria.

"The queen wants to taste what the people of Napoli eat," said Raffaele.

"Fine, fine. Then you must take this bottle. It is the finest in my shop, pressed from chilled olives that were carefully picked. Smell. You will think you were sitting under the tree from which it came. It will make your pizza sing."

"*Grazie*, Maria. It is perfect." And with that Raffaele took the bottle and put it in his sack.

Maria smiled as Raffaele left her shop.

Next he stopped at the pork store for some tasty sausage. Guiseppe was closing his shop for siesta, when everyone rested during the heat of the day; but when he saw Raffaele looking so frantic, he let him in. "What cannot wait until later, Raffaele?"

"I just need a bit of pork to add to my pizza for Queen Margherita," said Raffaele.

"Pizza with sausage for the queen? If you must make a pizza, at least put something on it fit for a queen, such as some prosciutto that's been cured, aged, and dried in the sweet air of Parma."

"Queen Margherita wants to eat the pizza that the people of Napoli eat."

"Well then, if it is the pizza that we eat, Napoli sausage you shall have," said Guiseppe with a hearty laugh.

And with that Raffaele took the sausage and put it in his sack. Guiseppe was still laughing as Raffaele left his shop.

Raffaele knew he must get back to his shop soon. The dough would be ready and people would now be lining up for a bite to eat. One last ingredient, he thought, and then he would get to work.

He went quickly down the street to the wharf. There he found Niccolo at his fish stand. "Niccolo, I am to make a pizza for the queen and would like to buy some little fish from you."

"Anchovies? No, Raffaele, you mustn't put anchovies on a pizza for the queen. Anchovies are too common. Maybe tuna. Tuna is finer and more appropriate for the queen."

"But the people of Napoli love the little fish on their pizza, and the queen wants the pizza that the people eat."

"Well, if that is what you want." And with that Raffaele took the package of anchovies from Niccolo. Before Niccolo could protest any further, Raffaele hurried from the wharf.

Raffaele rushed back, and people were already waiting for his pizza. There was Guiseppe from the pork store, Signora Libandi with little Alfonso, and Sebastiano, the barber, all impatiently waiting as Raffaele began to shape the risen dough and toss it.

They all watched as he spread the pizza with olive oil and added some of the little fish. He added some pine nuts, garlic, and cheese, and placed the pizza in the oven. That was Alfonso's favorite pizza.

Then Raffaele began on the next pizza. On that he spread some fresh tomatoes, garlic, and some more little fish. Sebastiano's mouth watered as he watched the pizza slide into the hot oven. The smell of garlic and of Raffaele's wonderful thin crust rose from the oven and drifted out the door of the shop. Soon more customers were in line. As each pizza came out, another went in until finally Raffaele had fed everyone.

It was not until five o'clock that Raffaele had time to start making the pizzas for the queen. He kneaded the dough and formed it into three little balls. Then he tossed each of the dough balls to shape his three pizzas.

On the dough of the first pizza he spread the green olive oil from Maria. Then he placed slices of fresh plum tomatoes from his garden, sprinkled oregano, and added just the right amount of garlic. He was sure the queen would like this one. Everyone loved his Pizza Marinara.

On the second he spread pieces of spicy sausage, slices of mozzarella di Bufala, and some leaves of freshly snipped basil. This was his favorite. Surely the queen would find it delicious.

On the third he would add the little fish that the people of Napoli loved. But where were the little fish? The plate was empty. Raffaele looked around the room only to find Meow-Meow stretched out asleep on the windowsill.

"Oh no, you didn't eat them, did you?" Raffaele looked at the cat's big belly and shook his head.

What would he do? He did not have time to go to the wharf again. And even if he did, Niccolo's stand was closed for the day.

Just as he was thinking that maybe two pizzas would be enough, he looked up to see the beautiful Italian flag blowing in the wind in the piazza. Raffaele looked at the flag's bold colors of green, white, and red against the bright blue sky. It was then that he knew what to add to the third pizza.

Quickly he cut up some more slices of red tomato and spread them on the dough. Then he added leaves of fresh green basil. Lastly he placed slices of white mozzarella di Bufala on top. The pizzas were finished. He slid them into the oven lined with rock from Mount Vesuvius.

Raffaele kept a careful eye on the pizzas as they cooked. He took them out of the oven just as the queen's messenger returned to take them to the castle.

"May I come with you to the castle?" asked Raffaele.

"Ahh, you are nervous that I might drop one?" The messenger laughed. "Her Majesty would be pleased to see the *pizzaiuolo* himself when she tastes the pizzas."

So together they made their way through the narrow streets and up the hill to the Castello di Capodimonte, where Queen Margherita was staying in Napoli. Raffaele was escorted through halls lined with the paintings of famous artists to the queen's dining room.

The queen was anxious to taste the pizzas. Their aroma had arrived before Raffaele and already filled the room. He set the pizzas before her.

First she tasted the pizza with olive oil, tomato, oregano, and garlic. Raffaele held his breath as she chewed the Pizza Marinara slowly. "Delicious," she remarked.

Next she lifted a slice with sausage, mozzarella, and basil to her lips. Raffaele watched nervously as a little string of cheese stretched from the pizza to her lips. It seemed endless until the queen took it into her fingers and popped it into her mouth.

"Also delicious." The queen giggled.

Before taking a bite of the last pizza, she looked at it for a moment. "Signore Esposito, you have captured the colors of our beloved flag on this pizza. I am sure to find it also delicious," she said.

Still Raffaele couldn't help but wonder what fine dishes the queen was used to eating. How did his pizza compare? He drew in his breath as the queen raised the slice of pizza to her lips. Before she had finished chewing completely, she took another bite. Then she exclaimed, "*Magnifico*, Signore Esposito."

Raffaele sighed with relief and bowed to Queen Margherita. The servants all clapped for Raffaele. The queen added, "Pizza for everyone!"

The next day was warm and sunny, like most June days in Napoli. The streets were busy with people selling cheese, fish, vegetables, and water. The smell of baking bread filled the air. Raffaele could feel the sun warming his face as he opened the pizzeria. Like every other morning Raffaele made his dough, kneaded it, and formed it into small balls that he would use for each pizza.

Word of Raffaele's success spread quickly through Napoli. By noon a line of customers already reached out the door, for today something else caught the customers' eyes on the menu: Pizza Margherita, a pizza fit for the queen, and the hungry bellies of Napoli.

Pizza Margherita

Pizza Dough

What you will need:

1 package yeast
1 teaspoon sugar
3/4 cup warm water
2 cups flour or more
1/2 teaspoon salt
1/8 cup olive oil

Measuring spoons
Measuring cups
Mixing bowl
Pastry board
Towel
Pizza pan
Grown-up help

1. Dissolve the yeast and sugar in warm water.
2. Mix the flour, salt, and olive oil together in a mixing bowl.
3. Put the flour mixture on a pastry board. Create a well in the center of the flour mixture. Pour the yeast mixture into the well and begin forming the dough with your hands.
4. Knead the dough until it is smooth and can be stretched. Add more warm water if necessary. If the dough seems sticky, add a little more flour.
5. Roll the dough into a ball and cover it with a towel. Let it rest for about 1 1/2 hours.
6. Now it is ready to be stretched into a pizza shell.

Topping

Ingredients for one pizza:

2 cups diced, peeled ripe tomatoes
1 large mozzarella di Bufala, sliced thinly
A handful of fresh basil leaves
Olive oil

1. Preheat oven to 500° F.

2. With well-floured hands, slap the dough onto a hard surface, such as a clean kitchen counter, to soften it.

3. Flatten the dough using your hands or a rolling pin to create the pizza shell. Be sure not to make any holes in it. Place it in a pizza pan.

4. Ask a grown-up to help dice the tomatoes and slice the mozzarella.

5. Drain the diced tomatoes and spoon them over the entire pizza shell.

6. Place thin slices of the mozzarella over the tomatoes. Drizzle some olive oil over the top.

7. Ask a grown-up to bake your pizza in the oven until the edge of the pizza shell rises and browns and the cheese is bubbly.

8. Scatter the fresh basil on top and serve.

If you need a reason to have a slice of pizza, February 9 has been declared International Pizza Day. It's also my birthday!

Author's Note

The first pizzeria was not Pietro e Basta Così, but Antica Pizzeria Port'Alba, which opened in Naples in 1830. Pietro e Basta Così became one of the most popular pizzerias after the invention of the Pizza Margherita, the cheese pizza we all know and love. But the story doesn't end in Naples; Gennaro Lombardi opened the first pizzeria in the United States in 1905. Today 93 percent of Americans eat at least one pizza per month, which averages out to 100 acres of pizzas each day or 350 slices per second. Pizza Margherita has found its place as the most popular pizza in the world.

Today at Pizza Brandi, formerly Pietro e Basta Così, in Naples, Italy, diners will find a framed certificate honoring Raffaele Esposito for the pizza he made for Queen Margherita on June 11, 1889.

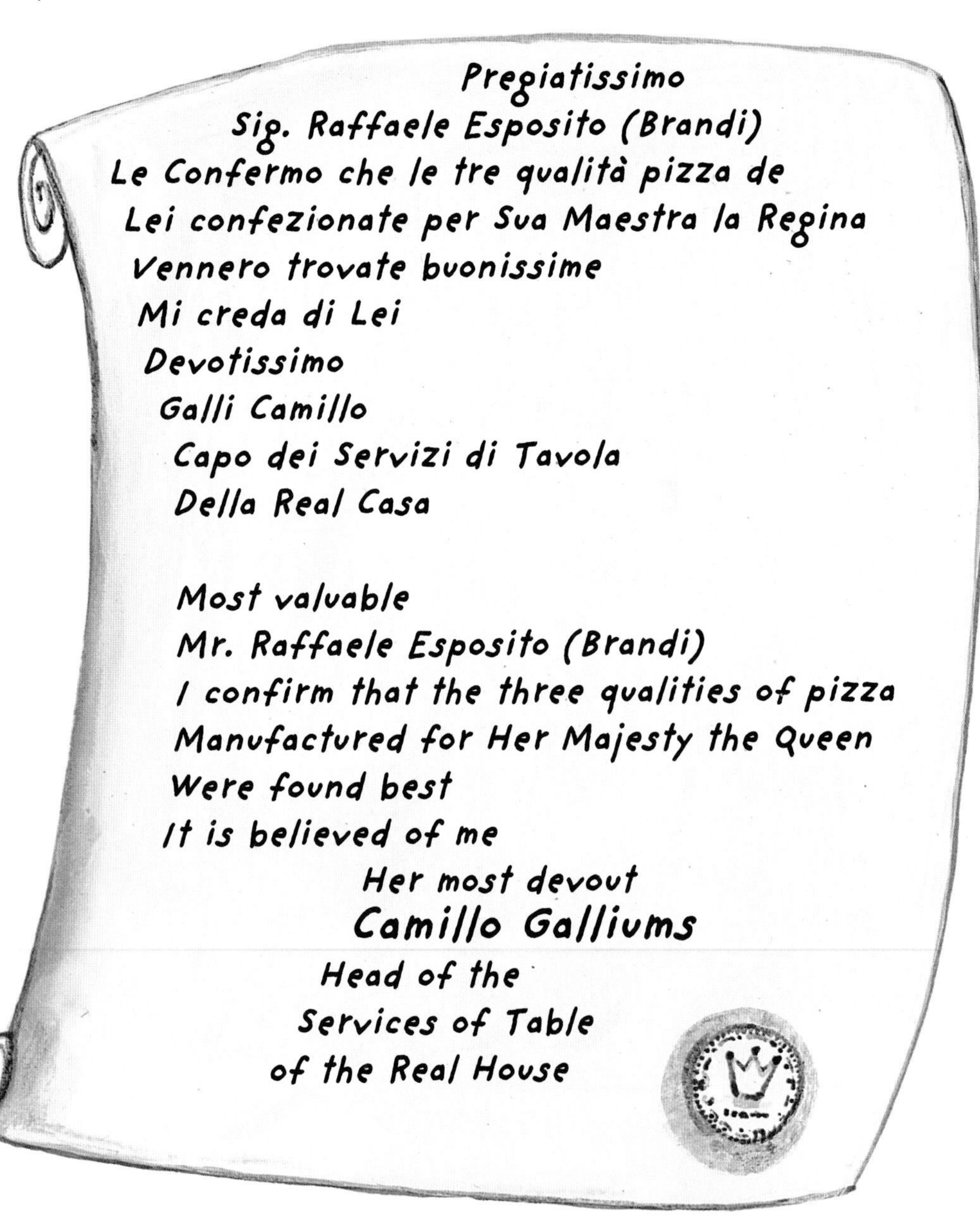
Pregiatissimo
Sig. Raffaele Esposito (Brandi)
Le Confermo che le tre qualità pizza de
Lei confezionate per Sua Maestra la Regina
Vennero trovate buonissime
Mi creda di Lei
Devotissimo
Galli Camillo
Capo dei Servizi di Tavola
Della Real Casa

Most valuable
Mr. Raffaele Esposito (Brandi)
I confirm that the three qualities of pizza
Manufactured for Her Majesty the Queen
Were found best
It is believed of me
Her most devout
Camillo Galliums
Head of the
Services of Table
of the Real House